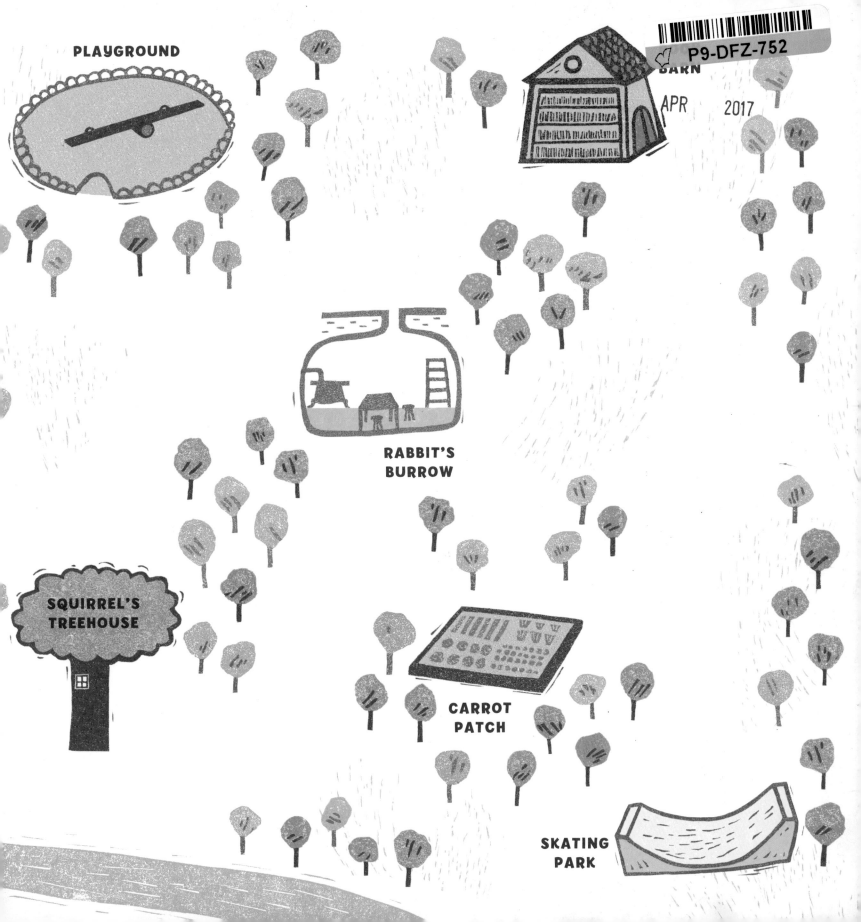

PLAYGROUND

BARN

APR 2017

RABBIT'S BURROW

SQUIRREL'S TREEHOUSE

CARROT PATCH

SKATING PARK

To Elsa and Georgina for helping me follow my dream

Clarion Books
3 Park Avenue
New York, New York 10016

Copyright © 2016 by Maria S. Costa

First published in the UK in 2016 by Oxford University Press,
Great Clarendon Street, Oxford OX2 6DP

Published in the U.S. in 2017

Clarion Books is an imprint of
Houghton Mifflin Harcourt Publishing Company.

www.hmhco.com

The illustrations in this book were done in linocut and digital media.
The text was set in Billy and Chaloops.

Library of Congress Cataloging-in-Publication Data
Names: Costa, Maria S., author, illustrator.
Title: How to find a friend / Maria S. Costa.
Description: Boston ; New York : Clarion Books, Houghton Mifflin Harcourt,
[2017] | "First published in the UK in 2016 by Oxford University
Press"--Copyright page. | Summary: A wistful blue squirrel and an athletic
red rabbit are each looking for a friend and missing each other by inches,
although helpful bugs are trying to steer them in the right direction.
Identifiers: LCCN 2016016158 | ISBN 9780544926783 (hardcover)
Subjects: | CYAC: Friendship--Fiction. | Squirrels--Fiction. |
Rabbits--Fiction. | Insects--Fiction.
Classification: LCC PZ7.1.C6745 Ho 2017 | DDC [E]--dc23
LC record available at https://lccn.loc.gov/2016016158

Manufactured in China
LEO 10 9 8 7 6 5 4 3 2 1
4500628600

How to find a friend

Maria S. Costa

Clarion Books
Houghton Mifflin Harcourt
Boston New York

When Squirrel moved into
her new treehouse,
she thought she might meet
a friend at the playground.

But she didn't.

Pssst!
I'll help Squirrel
find a friend!

When Rabbit moved
into his new burrow,
he thought the café
might be a good place
to meet a friend.

But it wasn't.

Hey!
I'll help Rabbit
find a friend!

What if I'm the only animal in the wood? wondered Squirrel.

But you're not!

What if I'm all alone
in the whole wide wood?
pondered Rabbit.

Look up there!

"It's such a shame that there's nobody around," said Rabbit.

"Really, I don't know where else to look," said Rabbit.

Try behind you!

"At least I have
my books for company,"
said Squirrel.

How about a rabbit for company?

**"If I keep myself busy, perhaps
I won't feel so lonely," said Rabbit.**

*If you keep going in this direction,
you definitely won't feel so lonely!*

"Oh, my!" said Squirrel.

ASH!

"What a surprise!"
said Rabbit.

"How come I never saw you before?" asked Squirrel.

"That's just what I was going to say!" Rabbit replied.

If only they'd listened to us!

Perhaps they don't speak Bug!

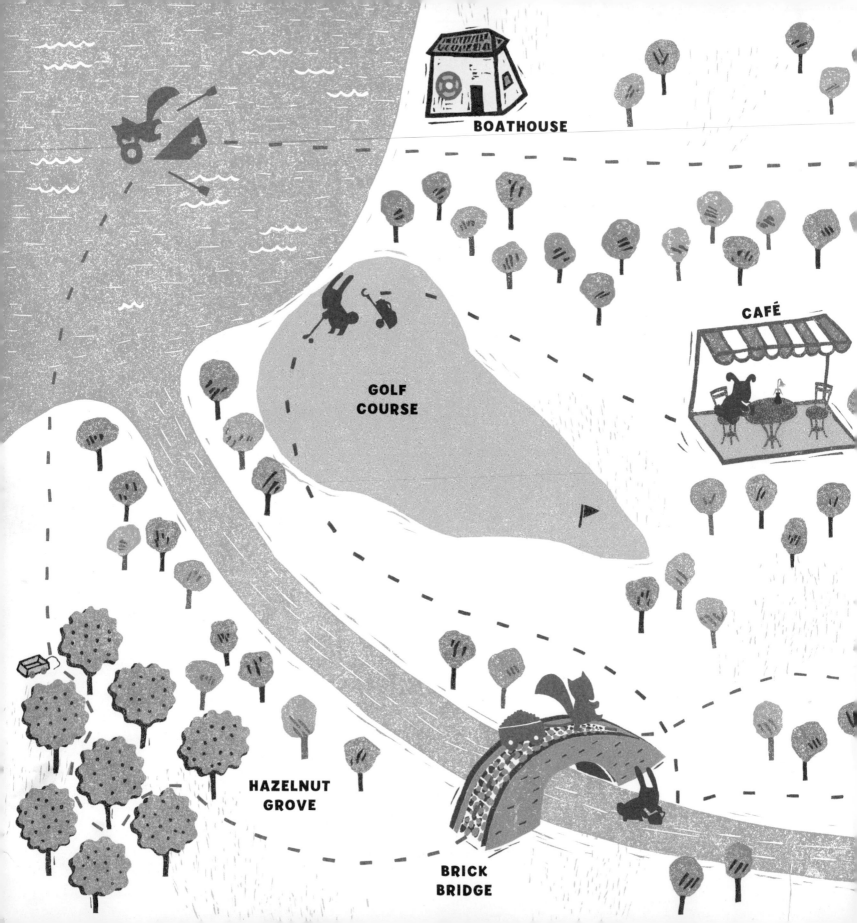

BOATHOUSE

CAFÉ

GOLF
COURSE

HAZELNUT
GROVE

BRICK
BRIDGE